Miss Bindergarten Celebrates the 100th DAY

# of Kindergarten

by JOSEPH SLATE
illustrated by ASHLEY WOLFF

PUFFIN BOOKS

"Tomorrow we celebrate," says Miss Bindergarten, "the 100th day of kindergarten."

"100 days of friends, 100 days of fun,
100 days of darling, dazzling, winning work you've done.
So remember that tomorrow all of you must bring
100 of some wonderful, one-hundred-full thing!"

That night—

Adam's fort is finished.

Brenda's
half asleep.

Christopher's
one hundred blocks
tumble in a heap.

Miss Bindergarten gets ready
for the 100th day of kindergarten.

94...95...96...

SPINACH
BEANS
CORN
PARTY
100 DAY PUNCH
10 CANS
LEMON-LIME POP
100 CHERRIES
100 ICE CUBES

The next morning—

Danny counts out cereal.

Emily fills a vase.

Franny draws a picture of her hundred-year-old face.

Miss Bindergarten gets ready

for the 100th day of kindergarten.

Gwen creates
a poster.

Henry claps
and cheers.

Ian brings a relative
who's lived a hundred years.

MAKE A HAT!
DECORATE AND ENJOY!
DAY 100

Miss Bindergarten gets ready
for the 100th day of kindergarten.

Jessie pokes her
polka dots.
Kiki carries tarts.

Lenny hugs a bagful of a hundred candy hearts.

Miss Bindergarten gets ready
for the 100th day of kindergarten.

COULD EA
100
PIZZAS
I COULD EAT
100
CRACKERS
KiKi
I COULD EAT
100
BANANAS
Gwen
I COULD EAT
100
GRAPES
URSULA
I COULD EAT
100
ICE CREAM CONES
CHRISTOPHER
I COULD EAT
100
PICKLES
Ian

Matty's bells go ding-a-ling.

Noah tootie-toots.

Ophelia's stuck with stickers from her hat down to her boots.

Miss Bindergarten gets ready

for the 100th day of kindergarten.

Patricia sorts her crayons.

Quentin revs toy cars.

Raffie lifts the lid up on
one hundred dinosaurs.

Miss Bindergarten is *almost* ready for the 100th day of kindergarten.

100 PINS

Sara checks
her ant farm.

Tommy flies
his kite.

Ursula's bag is heavy, but
Vicki's bunch is light.

Now Miss Bindergarten is all ready

for the 100th day of kindergarten.

Wanda whoops
and hollers.

Xavier shakes
his seeds.

Yolanda Pound and

Zachary Blair

boogie with their beads.

“Congratulations, kindergarten,”
says Miss Bindergarten.

“Without more delay...

let's celebrate the 100th day!”

I COULD EAT
100
FRENCH FRI
NOAH
HENRY
I COULD EAT
100
CANDIES
I COU
100
PEANU
BRENDA
1,2
buckle my shoe;
3,4
shut the door;
5,6
pick up sticks;
7,8
lay them straight;
9,10
a big, fat hen.
100 DAY
PUNCH

HEAVENLY
100 DAY HASH
Pick 10 pieces
from each bowl:
cereal-os, pretzels, marshmallows, nuts, sunflower seeds, raisins, choco chips, banana chips, cereal pillows, popcorn.
Adam's Fort
100
Popsicle sticks
Brenda's Chain
100
paper links
Christopher's Towers
100
plastic blocks
Gwen's Poster
prints of 100
fingers and toes
Henry's Sweater
100
buttons
Ian's Relative
100
years old
Jessie's Clothes
100
polka dots
Ophelia's Decorations
100 stickers
Patricia's Box
100 crayons
100
crayons
Quentin's Bag
100
toy cars
Raffie's Box
100
dinosaurs
Wanda's Lariat
100
rubber bands
Xavier's Packets
CORN
PUMPKINS
25 SEEDS
100
seeds
LET'S CELEBRATE THE 100TH DAY!
Miss B's Dress
100 bows

Danny's Design
100 cereal "stars"
Emily's Vase
100 flowers
Franny's Face
100 years old
100 DAY PUNCH
10 CANS LEMON-LIME POP
100 CHERRIES
100 ICE CUBES
MIX TOGETHER AND ENJOY!
Kiki's Treats
100 raspberry tarts
Lenny's Sack
100 candy hearts
Matty's Music
100 bells
Noah's Song
RAIN, RAIN!
100 notes
Sara's Farm
100 ants
Tommy's Kite
100 squares
Ursula's Bag
100 marbles
Vicki's Bunch
100 balloons
Yolanda's Necklaces
100 beads
Zachary's String
100 beads
Coco's Pile
100 staples

For Mickey, Mikey, Mark, Anna Maureen, and Annalea —J.S.

For Judy and Gerry, teachers and friends —A.W.

Our appreciation to Lynn Taylor, who introduced the celebration of 100 days in kindergarten in the 1981-82 Newsletter of the Center for Innovation in Education. Mrs. Taylor recently celebrated her 25th anniversary of teaching in primary grades in California and New Jersey. She was influenced by the late Mary Baratta-Lorton, whose theories on teaching children number concepts and math have been widely adopted. Mrs. Baratta-Lorton was director of early-childhood education at the California Center.—J.S. and A.W.

PUFFIN BOOKS
Published by the Penguin Group
Penguin Putnam Books for Young Readers,
345 Hudson Street, New York, New York 10014, U.S.A.
Penguin Books Ltd, 80 Strand, London WC2R ORL, England
Penguin Books Australia Ltd, 250 Camberwell Road, Camberwell, Victoria 3124, Australia
Penguin Books Canada Ltd, 10 Alcorn Avenue, Toronto, Ontario, Canada M4V 3B2
Penguin Books (N.Z.) Ltd, 182-190 Wairau Road, Auckland 10, New Zealand

Penguin Books Ltd, Registered Offices: Harmondsworth, Middlesex, England

First published in the United States of America by Dutton Children's Books, a division of Penguin Putnam Books for Young Readers, 1998
Published by Puffin Books, a division of Penguin Putnam Books for Young Readers, 2003

10 9 8 7 6 5 4 3 2 1

CIP Data is available.

Puffin Books ISBN 0-14-250005-4

Manufactured in China